Disney's Beauty and the Beast

The Beast's Story

Adapted by Laura Brooks
Illustrated by Ed Gutierrez and Serge Michaels

A Golden Book • New York
Western Publishing Company, Inc., Racine, Wisconsin 53404

Once there was a prince
who was spoiled and selfish.
One night a beggar woman
came to his castle.
She asked for shelter.
The prince would not let her in.

But the woman had magic powers.
She cast an evil spell and
turned the prince into a beast!

From that day on, the Beast
lived with his servants.
One night he was surprised
to find a stranger in his castle.
The stranger was sitting
in the Beast's chair!

"What are you doing here?"
roared the Beast.
"This is *my* castle.
And that is *my* chair."

"I was lost," said the stranger.
"Wolves were chasing me.
I needed a place to stay."

"I'll give you a place to stay!"
cried the Beast.
He locked the stranger
in the dungeon.

7

The next day another stranger
came to the castle.
This time it was a pretty girl.
The girl's name was Belle.
She was looking for her father.

The Beast saw Belle.
But he did not want
Belle to see him.

Belle soon found her father
in the dungeon.
Then she heard a noise.
"Is someone there?" she called.

11

The Beast stepped forward.

Belle was afraid of him.

But she wanted to save her father.

"Please let my father go," said Belle.

"I will," said the Beast.

"But you must stay here forever."

The Beast hoped Belle would
fall in love with him.
Only love would break the spell.
Then the Beast would turn
back into a prince.

Belle agreed to stay.

So the Beast sent her father home.

The Beast gave Belle
the finest room in the castle.

"You must join me for dinner!"
the Beast told Belle.
He did not know how to be polite.

Belle did not want to have
dinner with the Beast.
He was too rude.
So she stayed in her room.

The Beast waited for Belle.
"Where is she?" the Beast
asked his servants.
The servants did not answer.
They were too scared!

The Beast was angry.
He ran to Belle's room
and pounded on the door.

"Come out!" yelled the Beast.
"No!" cried Belle.
She would not open the door.

Later that night,
Belle was hungry.
She left her room and
went to the kitchen.

Then Belle looked around the castle.
The Beast had told her
she could not go into the West Wing.
But Belle went anyway.
She found the Beast's room.

23

The Beast found her there.
Now he was *really* angry.
"Get out!" he yelled.

Belle ran out of the castle.
She found her horse
and rode away.

But Belle was not safe yet.
Wolves attacked her and her horse!
Belle tried her best
to fight off the wolves,
but there were too many.

The Beast rushed to save her.
The wolves came after him!

The Beast won the fight.
Now Belle was safe.
But the Beast was wounded.

Belle wanted to help the Beast.
She took him back to the castle
and tended his wounds.
"Thank you for saving my life,"
she said.

The Beast was happy.
He was glad that Belle
had come back to the castle.

Maybe she would fall in love
with him after all!